Dear Parents:

Congratulations! Your child is takir̄ ~~~~~~
the first steps on an exciting journ ~~~~~~
The destination? Independent read ~~~~~~

STEP INTO READING® will help your child ge~~~~~~ ım offers
five steps to reading success. Each step includes fun stories and colorful
art or photographs. In addition to original fiction and books with favorite
characters, there are Step into Reading Non-Fiction Readers, Phonics Readers
and Boxed Sets, Sticker Readers, and Comic Readers—a complete literacy
program with something to interest every child.

Learning to Read, Step by Step!

Ready to Read   Preschool–Kindergarten
• big type and easy words • rhyme and rhythm • picture clues
For children who know the alphabet and are eager to
begin reading.

Reading with Help   Preschool–Grade 1
• basic vocabulary • short sentences • simple stories
For children who recognize familiar words and sound out
new words with help.

Reading on Your Own   Grades 1–3
• engaging characters • easy-to-follow plots • popular topics
For children who are ready to read on their own.

Reading Paragraphs   Grades 2–3
• challenging vocabulary • short paragraphs • exciting stories
For newly independent readers who read simple sentences
with confidence.

Ready for Chapters   Grades 2–4
• chapters • longer paragraphs • full-color art
For children who want to take the plunge into chapter books
but still like colorful pictures.

STEP INTO READING® is designed to give every child a successful
reading experience. The grade levels are only guides; children will progress
through the steps at their own speed, developing confidence in their reading.
The F&P Text Level on the back cover serves as another tool to help you
choose the right book for your child.

Remember, a lifetime love of reading starts with a single step!

To Su Monroe,
who loves snow days!
—C.R.

To my brothers.
Mamá beat us all in
our first snow fight ever.
—E.M.

Text copyright © 2018 by Candice Ransom
Cover art and interior illustrations copyright © 2018 by Erika Meza

Visit us on the Web!
StepIntoReading.com
rhcbooks.com

Educators and librarians, for a variety of teaching tools, visit us at RHTeachersLibrarians.com

Library of Congress Cataloging-in-Publication Data is available upon request.
ISBN 978-1-5247-2037-7 (trade) — ISBN 978-1-5247-2038-4 (lib. bdg.) —
ISBN 978-1-5247-2039-1 (ebook)

Printed in the United States of America
10 9 8 7 6 5 4 3 2
First Edition

This book has been officially leveled by using the F&P Text Level Gradient™ Leveling System.

STEP INTO READING®

STEP 1 READY TO READ

Snow Day!

by Candice Ransom
illustrated by Erika Meza

Random House 🏠 New York

First one flake,

then millions more!

Snow falls outside
our front door.

Cars are stuck.

No school today!
Now we can
go out and play.

Bunny hat—

on you, too cute!

Can not zip my coat.
Lost my boot!

Off we jump.

My feet sink deep.

Fluffy bushes
look like sheep.

Giant tracks.

Is it a bear?

Just a boy with
bright red hair!

Pull the sled
up that big hill.

Slide down too fast.

Take a spill!

Pile up snow
to build a fort.

Your wall is tall.

Mine is short.

You throw first.

Missed by a mile.

Splat!

Got your hat!

Made you smile.

Freezing hands,
cold, drippy nose.

Inside my boots,
chilly toes.

We sip cocoa
from a mug.
Blankets keep us
nice and snug.

Rumble! Roar!

Here comes the plow!

Sleep tight, street—
all clear now.

Hey! Wake up!
No time to play.

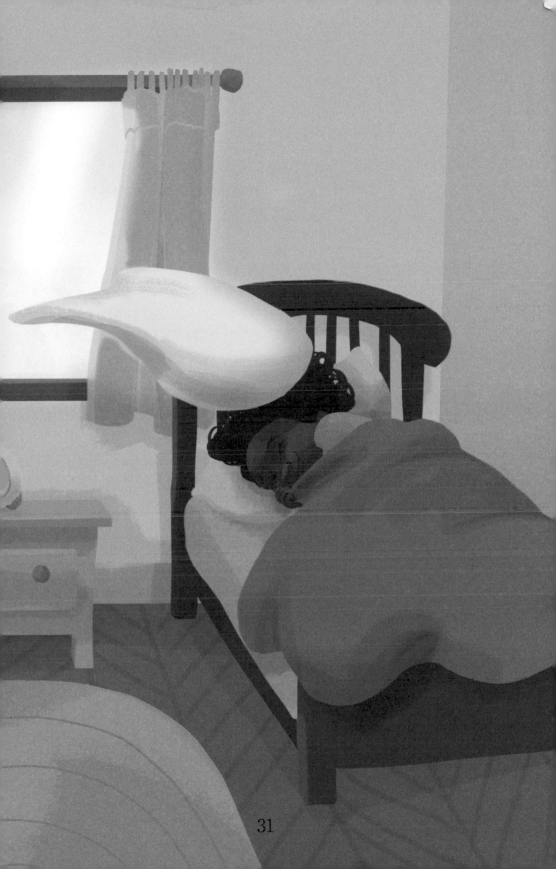

Back to school till
the next snow day!